ISBN number: 0-9780217-0-3
Greystoke Press Publishing: 0-9780217

Summary: Ogi, a little lake monster goes on a quest to become the next "Ogopogo"

1. Little Lake Monsters™ 2. Children's fiction 3. Faeries 4. Unicorn 5. Animals

32pp. and 8.5_X_11 inches

Original illustrations and digital art by Carole Thibault. Story by Carole Thibault.

Illustrations created with Bryce 5, Poser and Photoshop CS.

Book design with Adobe InDesign CS.

Published in Canada
Printed in Singapore, by Tien Wah Press
Book design: Carole Thibault

Dedication

I dedicate this book to my son, my friend and my inspiration.
I want to thank God for his continual guidance, and for being such a driving force in my life. Thank you to all the legendary lake monsters mentioned in this book. Ogopogo from Okanagan Lake, BC, Canada, Nessie from Loch Ness, Scotland, Champ from Lake Champlain, USA, Mempree from Lake Memphreemagog, Quebec, Canada and Issie from Lake Ikeda, Japan.

Special Thanks

To the city of Vernon, British Columbia, Canada, for the use of Ogopogo's name.

To Noel Westaway, for the 3D model of Ogopogo.

To Graham Gibbard and Brian Bakker,
-Refracted- Digital Art and Animation, for color conversion.

To my friend, Barbara Bertner for the final edits.

OGOPOGO

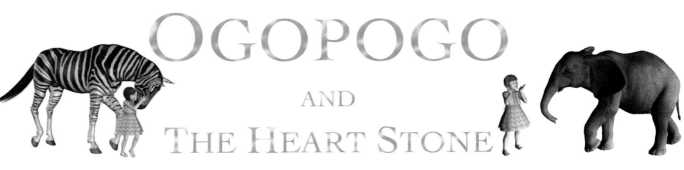

AND

THE HEART STONE

Written and illustrated by Carole Thibault

GREYSTOKE PRESS

PUBLISHING

Lost in time and hidden from men, exists the magical and mystical land known as the 'valley of pure hearts'. This valley is long and wide, surrounded by misty hills and snow-capped mountains that stretch to the sky. Pristine forests and flowering meadows are alive with animals and creatures of all kinds, playing and living together in peace and harmony. Cascading waterfalls and crystal clear streams empty into a deep blue lake.

The far end of the lake disappears into a large cave at the bottom of a huge mountain. This is the passageway that leads to the world of man. At the other end of the passage stands a large boulder, blocking the way and hiding it from mankind. This is the 'Heart Stone' and it can only be passed by those who are pure of heart.

The guardian and protector of this lost valley is a legendary lake monster. Every few hundred years, a new young guardian is chosen.

This is the story of the little lake monster named Ogi who is chosen to become the new 'OGOPOGO'. To prove his worth, Ogi is given a quest. He must find a human with a pure heart and bring that person back to his valley.

Ogi was accompanied to the entrance of the world of man by his father, Ogopogo. Swimming together through the cave leading to the outside world, Ogi intently listened to Ogopogo's stories and counsel.

Ogopogo said, "Take this necklace. When you find a human with a pure heart it will radiate a rainbow of colors. Be safe, little one and trust in the stone."

Ogi could hardly rest the night Ogopogo told him of his quest. Excitement kept his eyes open and his mind alert for a long time, but he finally fell into a deep and relaxing sleep. Ogi awoke before the sun rose and was excited that this was the day to begin his adventure. In one leap, Ogi dove into the gleaming lake inside the cave and swam toward the heart stone.

Ogi had never entered the world of man alone before and he felt both fear and excitement. Deep within the cave he came upon the heart stone. It glowed in splendid colors, lighting up the entrance to man's world and allowing him to pass.

Summer was almost over, yet the morning was warm. Ogi glanced out upon the lake at the cave entrance and observed boats on the water. He remembered his father's instructions well and to stay underwater when humans were nearby. Boats were to be avoided; he had learned this from noticing the scars on Ogopogo's back.

As Ogi entered the world of man he noticed that his close friend Tassina, the little faerie, had accompanied him. She would never stray far from Ogi as she was to look out for him during his quest.

Tassina exclaimed, "See the marsh ahead? There lives a beaver named Buster. He is a close friend of your father's."

Ogi called softly as they neared the beaver's lodge. Buster was happy to meet him and invited him in for a bite to eat. Over breakfast Ogi listened to many stories about the adventures his father and Buster had over the years. Soon Ogi exclaimed, "I must excuse myself and begin my quest."

Ogi thanked Buster for his hospitality and kindness.

Giving Ogi his blessing Buster said, "Be cautious, my little friend. Have faith, and you will find what you are looking for."

As soon as Ogi left Buster's lodge, he dove deep into the lake and heard familiar voices. Several little lake monsters from other hidden valleys had gathered in Okanagan Lake.

There was Nessie from Loch Ness, Champ from Lake Champlain, Memphree from Lake Memphreemagog and Memphree's twin Issie from Lake Ikeda in Japan.

"What are you guy's doing here?" A surprised Ogi asked.

Little Nessie was the first to reply. "We heard that you are on a journey to find a human being with a pure heart and we wondered if could join you?"

"Of course!" Ogi replied with a huge smile. He welcome the companionship of his dear friends.

Ogi felt his spirit soar and was now convinced that with the support of his best friends he would find a pure-hearted human. For the remainder of the day they searched, played and enjoyed each other's company.

By sunset the little lake monsters were weary and hungry.

Ogi said, "I know of a secluded beach not far from here, it will be a safe place to rest."

The beach was lovely. It was a quiet and sandy spot filled with wild flowers and weeping willows. There was also plenty to eat. After eating their fill they all curled up together under a full moon for a much needed rest.

Ogi was awakened by noises coming from nearby. Although being a little afraid, he quietly moved toward the sounds. After a few moments he observed a small child crying and alone. He soon returned to the others and woke them.
"There is a little child nearby. What do we do?" Ogi whispered.

The little lake monsters cautiously made their way into the lake. They wanted to help but were afraid. They swam quietly, bobbing in the waves and watching. As they neared the beach they noticed a shipwreck on the shore.

Sitting on a large boulder at the edge of the lake was a young girl, crying. Ogi noticed that the child was perhaps five or six in human years. Finally Ogi said, " We must do something to help."

His voice startled the little girl. She leaped to her feet, abruptly lost her balance, and fell into the lake. Ogi was by her side in seconds, catching her by her dress and lifting her out of the water. As he carefully placed her on the shore he felt his necklace begin to pulsate and glow.

When the others witness the brilliant colorful lights radiating from Ogi's necklace, they all shouted joyfully, "It's her! It's her! She must be the one!"

The little girl sat on the beach trembling as Ogi tried to console her, "Don't fear, we mean you no harm," he said.
"Yes," agreed Nessie, "we are here to help you."
"What is your name," Ogi asked, "and why are you so sad?"
The little girl looked at Ogi's glowing necklace and said, "My name is Caitlin and I am lost," she said, sobbing.
"Where are your parents?" Asked Issie.
"I don't know," she responded, "we were on the lake when a terrible storm overturned our boat. I awoke here alone and hungry." She cried, rubbing her tear-stained eyes.

Ogi glanced at his friends and said to Caitlin, "I know a valley not far from here where the food is plentiful. Would you like to come there with us?"

"I will if you agree to help me find my way home," Caitlin replied.

"We promise!" They all shouted together.

Champ raised an eyebrow and said, "we must leave now if we want to make it back by nightfall."

"Caitlin, will you do me the honor to ride with me, to my valley?" Ogi asked.

"Yes," Caitlin responded, as she tentatively waded into the water towards Ogi. She climbed onto Ogi's back and settled down.

Ogi began swimming with long smooth glides. They traveled all day. As they neared the cave entrance, Memphree swam to Ogi and with alarm in his voice, exclaimed, "There is trouble ahead. It could be a search party looking for the family!"

Ogi thought for a moment, then calmly said, "Can you hold your breath underwater for a little while, Caitlin? Just hold on to my fin."

Caitlin nodded and held on tight as she drew in a deep breath. Ogi went under the water in a shallow dive and passed the first boats.

Ogi plunged once more and they were soon clear of the boats. They left man's world and passed through the heart stone.

Upon entering Ogi's valley, her sadness was replaced with joy. Caitlin was amazed at the valley's beauty.

"Did you sense the power of the heart stone?" Ogi asked.

"I did when we swam past it. That was fun. Can we do it again?" Caitlin giggled.

Ogi smiled and said, "You felt the healing power the stone. You are now connected to the energy of pure love. From now on, like all of us, you will shine with an inner light and radiate kindness to all."

It wasn't long before Ogopogo was informed of their arrival. The old guardian joined Ogi and embraced him with great affection.

"I have discovered a child with a pure heart," Ogi said proudly. "This is Caitlin!"

Ogopogo leaned down and gently tapped Caitlin's head. "I am very happy to meet you, little one. Welcome to our valley."

Caitlin gazed up at him with wide-eye wonder. Ogopogo was at least ten times larger than Ogi.

Standing by Ogopogo's side, Caitlin said with fear in her voice, "There is a tiger coming towards us."

"Don't worry," Ogi reassured her, "all the creatures of the valley live in peace with one another. We all feed on the vegetation the valley has to offer."

By this time, various animals of the valley had gathered. Blossom, a noble Unicorn, approached Caitlin and gently dropped an apple by her feet, which Caitlin quickly ate.

Blossom bowed down and said, "Climb on, I will carry you around our beautiful valley."

Caitlin climbed on, and held onto Blossom's long and silky mane. Blossom gently walked around the valley, introducing Caitlin to everyone.

Caitlin spent a full day playing with the various inhabitants of the valley. She was particularly delighted in monkeying around with a family of gorillas.

Caitlin was astonished by the wide assortment of animals and creatures living in harmony with one another. She could hardly believe her eyes when she witness a little fawn curled up by a majestic tiger. Soon Caitlin began to tire and found herself resting her head on Blossom's neck, drifting in and out of sleep.

Shaka, the elephant matriarch, quietly approached Blossom. With her trunk she carefully lifted Caitlin and delicately laid her upon a down-covered nest.

Ogi curled up beside her and both slept through the next morning. Waking up by Ogi's side, Caitlin knew she had not dreamed this awesome adventure.

Stretching, she said, "Ogi, I am so happy you have brought me here. I have made several new friends and I have seen things I would never have believed existed. Thank you. I also feel a little sad, I really miss my mommy and daddy."

Ogi replied, "Don't be sad, little one. You will soon be reunited with your family, just as we promised."

The sun rose high above the mountains, filling the valley with wondrous light. Soon the rays found Caitlin, and she was filled with amazing warmth and began to glow. All the creatures of the valley witness the brightness coming from within her, and all knew that she was now part of them forever.

Surrounded by all her new friends, Caitlin knew it was time to go home. Ogi was getting ready to take her back to the world of man. Meanwhile, Caitlin strolled about and accepted food her new friends gathered for her journey back.

"Climb on, little one, we must return at once and find a search party," Ogi said with a lump in his throat.

Ogi felt sadness in his heart for the very first time. He knew he would miss Caitlin dearly, but he was comforted by the thought that they would meet again.

Caitlin, also knew she would miss all of her new friends. Saying goodbye wasn't easy. She approached Ogi and wrapped her arms around his neck and said with tears in her eyes, "Ogi, I will miss you most of all."

Caitlin climbed onto Ogi's back and together they returned to her world. At sundown Ogi brought Caitlin to a beach, where they found one of the search party.

Soon Caitlin and the little lake monsters would began new journeys of their own, and help the world re-connect with love and kindness.